The Mountain That Loved a Bird

by Alice McLerran
Pictures by Eric Carle

PICTURE BOOK STUDIO

There was once a mountain made of bare stone.
It stood alone in the middle of a desert plain. No plant grew on its hard
slopes, nor could any animal, bird or insect live there.

The sun warmed the mountain and the wind chilled it, but the only
touch the mountain knew was the touch of rain or snow.
There was nothing more to feel.

All day and all night the mountain looked only at the sky, watching for
the movement of the billowing clouds. It knew the path of the sun that
crossed the sky by day, and the course of the moon that crossed the sky
by night. On clear nights, it watched the slow wheeling of the far-off stars.
There was nothing more to see.

But then one day a small bird appeared. She flew in a circle above the mountain, then landed on a ledge to rest and preen her feathers. The mountain felt the dry grasp of her tiny claws on the ledge; it felt the softness of her feathered body as she sheltered herself against its side. The mountain was amazed, for nothing like this had ever come to it from the sky before.

"Who are you?" the mountain asked. "What is your name?"

"I am a bird," replied the other. "My name is Joy, and I come from distant lands, where everything is green. Every spring I fly high into the air, looking for the best place to build my nest and raise my children. As soon as I have rested I must continue my search."

"I have never seen anything like you before," said the mountain. "Must you go on? Couldn't you just stay here?"

Joy shook her head. "Birds are living things," she explained. "We must have food and water. Nothing grows here for me to eat; there are no streams from which I could drink."

"If you cannot stay here, will you come back again some day?" asked the mountain.

Joy thought for a while. "I fly long distances," she said, "and I have rested on many mountains. No other mountain has ever cared whether I came or went, and I should like to return to you. But I could only do so in the spring before I build my nest, and because you are so far from food and water I could only stay a few hours."

"I have never seen anything like you before," repeated the mountain. "Even if it were only for a few hours, it would make me happy to see you again."

"There is one more thing you should know," said Joy. "Mountains last forever, but birds do not. Even if I were to visit you every spring of my life, there might be only a few visits. Birds do not live very many years."

"It will be very sad when your visits stop," said the mountain, "but it would be even sadder if you fly away now and never return."

Joy sat very still, nestled against the side of the mountain. Then she began to sing a gentle, bell-like song, the first music the mountain had ever heard. When she had finished her song, she said, "Because no mountain has ever before cared whether I came or went, I will make you a promise. Every spring of my life, I will return to greet you, and fly above you, and sing to you. And since my life will not last forever, I will give to one of my daughters my own name, Joy, and tell her how to find you. And she will name a daughter Joy also, and tell her how to find you. Each Joy will have a daughter Joy, so that no matter how many years pass, you will always have a friend to greet you and fly above you and sing to you."

The mountain was both happy and sad. "I still wish you could stay," it said, "but I am glad you will return."

"Now I must go," said Joy, "for it is a long way to the lands that have food and water for me. Goodbye until next year." She soared off, her wings like feathered fans against the sun. The mountain watched her until she disappeared into the distance.

Year after year, when every spring came, a small bird flew to the mountain, singing, "I am Joy, and I have come to greet you." And for a few hours, the bird would fly above the mountain, or nestle against its side, singing. At the end of each visit, the mountain always asked, "Isn't there some way you could stay?" And Joy always answered, "No, but I will return next year."

Each year the mountain looked forward more and more to Joy's visit; each year it grew harder and harder to watch her go. Ninety-nine springs came and went in this way. On the hundredth spring, when it was time for Joy to leave, the mountain asked once more, "Isn't there some way you could stay?" Joy answered, as she always did, "No, but I will return next year." The mountain watched as she disappeared into the sky, and suddenly its heart broke. The hard stone cracked, and from the deepest part of the mountain tears gushed forth and rolled down the mountainside in a stream.

The next spring a small bird appeared, singing, "I am Joy, and I have come to greet you." This time the mountain did not reply. It only wept, thinking of how soon she would have to leave, and of all the long months before she would come again. Joy rested on her ledge, and looked at the stream of tears. Then she flew above the mountain, and sang as she always had. When it was time for her to go, the mountain still wept. "I will return next year," said Joy softly, and she flew away.

When the next spring came, Joy
returned, carrying in her beak a small
seed. The mountain still wept a stream
of tears. Joy carefully tucked the seed
into a crack in the hard stone, close
to the stream so that it would stay
moist. Then she flew above the
mountain, and sang to it. Seeing that
the mountain was still unable to speak,
she flew away once more.

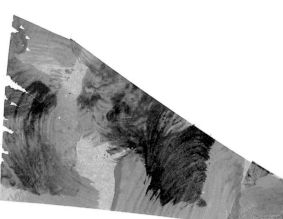

During the weeks that followed, the seed in the crack of the rock began to send down tiny roots. The roots reached into the hard stone, little by little spreading into yet smaller cracks, breaking through the hardness. As the roots found water in the cracks, and drew food from the softening stone, a shoot rose from the seed into the sunlight and unfolded tiny green leaves. The mountain, however, was still deep in sorrow, blind with tears. It did not notice a plant so small.

The next spring Joy brought another seed, and the spring after that another. She placed each one in a protected place near the stream of tears, and sang to the mountain. The mountain still only wept.

Years passed in this way, the roots of new plants softening the stone near the stream of tears. As softened stone turned to soil, moss began to grow in sheltered corners. Grasses and little flowering plants sprouted in hollows near the stream. Tiny insects, carried to the mountain by the winds, scurried among the leaves.

Meanwhile, the roots of the very first seed went deeper and deeper into the heart of the mountain. Above the ground, what had started as a tiny shoot was growing into the trunk of a young tree, its branches holding green leaves out to the sun. At last, the mountain felt the roots reaching down like gentle fingers, filling and healing the cracks in its heart. Sorrow faded away, and the mountain began to notice the changes that had been taking place. Seeing and feeling so many wonderful new things, the mountain's tears changed to tears of happiness.

Each year Joy returned, bringing another seed. Each year, more streams ran laughing down the mountain's sides, and the ground watered by the new streams grew green with trees and other plants.

Now that the mountain no longer wept with sorrow, it began to ask once more, "Isn't there some way you could stay?" But Joy still answered, "No, but I will return next year."

More years passed, and the streams carried life far out into the plain surrounding the mountain, until finally, as far as the mountain could see, everything was green. From lands beyond the horizon, small animals began to come to the mountain. Watching these living things find food and shelter on its slopes, the mountain suddenly felt a surge of hope. Opening its deepest heart to the roots of the trees, it offered them all its strength. The trees stretched their branches yet higher toward the sky, and hope ran like a song from the heart of the mountain into every tree leaf.

And sure enough, when the next spring came,
Joy flew to the mountain carrying not a seed,
but a slender twig. Straight to the tallest tree
on the mountain she flew, to the tree that had
grown from the very first seed. She placed the
twig on the branch in which she would build her nest.
"I am Joy," she sang, "and I have come to stay."

LIBRARY OF CONGRESS CATALOGING IN PUBLICATION DATA
McLerran, Alice.
The mountain that loved a bird.
Summary: A beautiful bird brings life to a lonely, barren mountain.
[1. Birds—Fiction. 2. Mountain—Fiction]
I. Carle, Eric, ill. II. Title.
PZ7.M47872Mo 1985   [E]   85-9391
ISBN 0-88708-000-6

Ask your bookseller for these other PICTURE BOOK STUDIO books
illustrated by Eric Carle:
THE GREEDY PYTHON by Richard Buckley
THE FOOLISH TORTOISE by Richard Buckley
A HOUSE FOR HERMIT CRAB
HAVE YOU SEEN MY CAT?
ROOSTER'S OFF TO SEE THE WORLD
PAPA, PLEASE GET THE MOON FOR ME
THE TINY SEED
ALL AROUND US